Note to parents, carers and teachers

Read it yourself is a series of modern stories, favourite characters and traditional tales written in a simple way for children who are learning to read. The books can be read independently or as part of a guided reading session.

Each book is carefully structured to include many high-frequency words vital for first reading. The sentences on each page are supported closely by pictures to help with understanding, and to offer lively details to talk about.

The books are graded into four levels that progressively introduce wider vocabulary and longer stories as a reader's ability and confidence grows.

Ideas for use

- Begin by looking through the book and talking about the pictures. Has your child heard this story before?

- Help your child with any words he does not know, either by helping him to sound them out or supplying them yourself.

- Developing readers can be concentrating so hard on the words that they sometimes don't fully grasp the meaning of what they're reading. Answering the puzzle questions at the end of the book will help with understanding.

For more information and advice on Read it yourself and book banding, visit www.ladybird.com/readityourself

Book Band 7

Level 2 is ideal for children who have received some reading instruction and can read short, simple sentences with help.

Special features:

Frequent repetition of main story words and phrases

Ben and Holly are playing with their friends.

"What have you got there, Gaston?" says Holly.

"It's a toy arm!" says Ben.

Short, simple sentences

Large, clear type

Then Ben goes to bed. But the robot will not stop.

"Must tidy up," says the robot.

"This robot is strange," says the king.

Careful match between story and pictures

Educational Consultant: Geraldine Taylor
Book Banding Consultant: Kate Ruttle

LADYBIRD BOOKS

UK | USA | Canada | Ireland | Australia
India | New Zealand | South Africa

Ladybird Books is part of the Penguin Random House group of companies
whose addresses can be found at global.penguinrandomhouse.com.

ladybird.com

Published by Ladybird Books Ltd, 2015
001

This book is based on the
TV Series 'Ben and Holly's Little Kingdom'
'Ben and Holly's Little Kingdom' is created by
Neville Astley and Mark Baker
Ben and Holly's Little Kingdom © Astley Baker Davies Ltd/
Entertainment One UK Ltd, 2008.

www.littlekingdom.co.uk

Printed in China

A CIP catalogue record for this book is
available from the British Library

978-0-241-19898-8

The Toy Robot

Adaptation written by Ellen Philpott
Based on the TV series 'Ben and Holly's Little Kingdom'
'Ben and Holly's Little Kingdom' is created by
Neville Astley and Mark Baker

Ben and Holly are playing with their friends.

"What have you got there, Gaston?" says Holly.

"It's a toy arm!" says Ben.

"Look!" says Holly.
"A toy robot!"

"We can fix it," says Ben.

"Then what will it do?"
says Holly.

"Toy robots just walk and say *bleep, bleep*," says Ben.

The elves fix the robot.
They put his arm back.

"Now get the key," says Ben.

"There is no key!"
says Holly.

Holly makes a magic key.
It makes the robot go!

"You are my master,"
he says to Ben.

"Toy robots should just
say *bleep bleep*!" says the
Wise Old Elf.

13

Then the robot grabs the Wise Old Elf!

"Put him down!" says Ben.

"Yes, Master," says the robot.

"This robot is strange," says the Wise Old Elf.

Ben and Holly play
with their robot.

"It will do what you say,
Ben!" says Holly.

So Ben says, "Tidy up, robot."

"Yes, Master," says the robot.

Then Ben goes to bed.
But the robot will not stop.

"Must tidy up," says
the robot.

"This robot is strange,"
says the king.

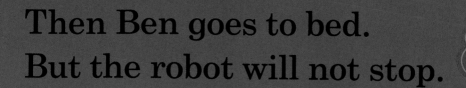

The king and queen go to bed.
But the robot will not stop.

"Must tidy up," he says.

Then the robot grabs
the king and queen!

"Ben is my master," says the robot.

"Right. Get Ben!" says the king.

So Ben goes back to the king with his elf friends.

23

Just then, the magic stops... and the robot stops!

"The magic key makes him strange," says Ben.

Then Gaston walks up
to Holly.

"What have you got there,
Gaston?" she says.

It is the right robot key!

The elves put the right key in, and the robot walks.

Bleep, bleep!

"Now this is what toy robots should do!" says Ben.

How much do you remember about Ben and Holly's Little Kingdom: The Toy Robot? Answer these questions and find out!

- **What does Gaston find?**

- **What does Holly make with magic?**

- **What are toy robots supposed to say?**

- **Who does the robot call Master?**

Look at the pictures and match them to the story words.

Ben

Holly

Wise Old Elf

Gaston

robot

Tick the books you've read!

Level 2

Big Machines · Camping Trip · THE ANGRY OWL · Beauty and the Beast · Chicken Licken · The Monster Next Door · The Gingerbread Man · Wild Animals · School Bus Trip

Little Red Riding Hood · Nature Trail · Sports Day · Pirate School · Rumpelstiltskin · Sleeping Beauty · Dom's Dragon · Superhero Max · TREEHOUSE RESCUE

Sly Fox and Red Hen · The Tale of JEMIMA PUDDLE-DUCK · The Three Little Pigs · Why Lion ROARRRS! · The Big Race · Town Mouse and Country Mouse · Topsy and Tim Go to London

Level 3

Puss in Boots · ANGRY BIRDS MATILDA SAVES THE DAY · Sharks · Thumbelina · Aladdin · YOU won't like this present as much as I DO! · The Elves and the Shoemaker · Hansel and Gretel · Harry and the Bucketful of Dinosaurs

Jack and the Beanstalk · Fur on Music Island · Poppet Stows Away · Rapunzel · The Red Knight · The Jungle Book · Roxy and the Great Escape · ANGRY BIRDS BOMB'S BEST BIRTHDAY · ANGRY BIRDS CHUCK